This book belongs to:

_____

Text copyright © 2006 by Callaway & Kirk Company LLC.
Illustrations copyright © 1997 by Callaway & Kirk Company LLC.

All rights reserved. Published by Scholastic Inc. in association with Callaway & Kirk Company LLC.
Miss Spider and all related characters are trademarks and/or registered trademarks of Callaway & Kirk Company LLC.
SCHOLASTIC, CARTWHEEL BOOKS, and associated logos are trademarks and/or registered trademarks of Scholastic Inc.

150-4681

ISBN: 0-439-83306-X

11 10 9 8 7 6 5 4 3   6 7 8 9 10/0

Printed in Mexico
This edition first printing, May 2006

The paintings in this book are oil on paper.

Miss Spider's New Car

paintings and verse by David Kirk

Cartwheel
·B·O·O·K·S·®

Callaway Arts & Entertainment

"Mom writes that we should meet for tea," Miss Spider said. "Please come with me!"

Poor Holley said,
"We must not go.
There are monsters
on the way, you know!"

Miss Spider smiled
and bit her lip.
"We'll buy a car
to make the trip."

She loved an egg sedan they found.
But Holley said, "Let's shop around."

"You'll want a car with lots of speed. This bumblebee is what you need."

Miss Spider said, "It's fun to shop!"
Poor Holley shouted, "Stop! Stop! Stop!"

"This buggy is slower than a snail.
And it leaves a yucky, mucky trail."

"Perhaps this hopping car would do?
Jump up, my friend. There's room for two!"

"Or better yet, your car should fly.
The view is nicest from the sky!"

Meg's
Wings
n'
Things

"This matchbox car has lots of room, but watch out for that tree!" KABLOOM

"My egg car must be gone by now.
I didn't earn one anyhow."

They rushed back to Bub Bumble's lawn.
And sure enough, the car was gone.

But it was not the way it seemed.
I had the moth buy it," Holley beamed.

So now they're off,
but look—a note!

M om is buying them
a brand-new boat.

11/19   12   7/19

8/22   12   7/19